ABOUT THE BANK STREET READY-TO-READ SERIES

More than seventy-five years of educational research, innovative teaching, and quality publishing have earned The Bank Street College of Education its reputation as America's most trusted name in early childhood education.

Because no two children are exactly alike in their development, the Bank Street Ready-to-Read series is written on three levels to accommodate the individual stages of reading readiness of children ages three through eight.

○ *Level 1:* GETTING READY TO READ (Pre-K–Grade 1)
Level 1 books are perfect for reading aloud with children who are getting ready to read or just starting to read words or phrases. These books feature large type, repetition, and simple sentences.

○ *Level 2:* READING TOGETHER (Grades 1–3)
These books have slightly smaller type and longer sentences. They are ideal for children beginning to read by themselves who may need help.

○ *Level 3:* I CAN READ IT MYSELF (Grades 2–3)
These stories are just right for children who can read independently. They offer more complex and challenging stories and sentences.

All three levels of The Bank Street Ready-to-Read books make it easy to select the books most appropriate for your child's development and enable him or her to grow with the series step by step. The levels purposely overlap to reinforce skills and further encourage reading.

We feel that making reading fun is the single most important thing anyone can do to help children become good readers. We hope you will become part of Bank Street's long tradition of learning through sharing.

The Bank Street College
of Education

To Cheré and Roy
— J.O.

To my cats, Paddy and John,
who were my technical advisors
on this book
— C.N.

For a free color catalog describing Gareth Stevens' list of high-quality books and multimedia programs, call 1-800-542-2595 (USA) or 1-800-461-9120 (Canada). Gareth Stevens Publishing's Fax: (414) 225-0377.
See our catalog, too, on the World Wide Web: http://gsinc.com

Library of Congress Cataloging-in-Publication Data

Oppenheim, Joanne.
  Do you like cats? / by Joanne Oppenheim; illustrated by Carol Newsom.
    p. cm. -- (Bank Street ready-to-read)
    Summary: Simple rhyming text and illustrations present different kinds of cats and their behavior.
    ISBN 0-8368-1757-5 (lib. bdg.)
    [1. Cats--Fiction. 2. Stories in rhyme.] I. Newsom, Carol, ill.
  II. Title. III. Series.
  PZ8.3.0615Dm 1998
  [E]--dc21   97-30215

This edition first published in 1998 by
Gareth Stevens Publishing
1555 North RiverCenter Drive, Suite 201
Milwaukee, Wisconsin 53212 USA

© 1993 by Byron Preiss Visual Publications, Inc. Text © 1993 by Bank Street College of Education. Illustrations © 1993 by Carol Newsom and Byron Preiss Visual Publications, Inc.

Published by arrangement with Bantam Doubleday Dell Books for Young Readers, a division of Bantam Doubleday Dell Publishing Group, Inc., New York, New York.
All rights reserved.

Bank Street Ready To Read ™ is a registered U.S. trademark of the Bank Street Group and Bantam Doubleday Dell Books For Young Readers, a division of Bantam Doubleday Dell Publishing Group, Inc.

Printed in Mexico

1 2 3 4 5 6 7 8 9 02 01 00 99 98

Do You Like Cats?

by Joanne Oppenheim
Illustrated by Carol Newsom

A Byron Preiss Book

Gareth Stevens Publishing
MILWAUKEE

Do you like cats—
short-haired sleek cats,
playing-hide-and-seek cats,

slink-around-the-house cats,
pounce-and-catch-a-mouse cats?

Do you like long-haired cats—
cats with bushy tails and tufts,
cats with paws of silky puffs?

Short fur,
long fur—
what kind of cat
do you prefer?

Would you like a tabby cat,
all striped in gray and black?

8

Or would you choose a calico,
with patches on its back?

How about a Siamese,
born as white as snow?

Did you know that Siamese
change color as they grow?

Would you pick a tail-less Manx?
A silvery Russian Blue?

A gray Maltese?
A red Burmese?
Is one of these
for you?

Do you like stray cats —
roaming-night-and-day cats,
nameless-on-their-own cats,
haven't-got-a-home cats,
independent lone cats?

Do you like these?

Alley cats, street cats,
scrounging-food-to-eat cats,
living-by-their-wits cats,
landing-on-their-feet cats –

do you like these?

Do you like pet cats—
stay-at-home-and-play cats,
like-to-have-their-way cats,
napping-through-the-day cats?

18

Give them a name,
give them a dish,
and give them the space
to do as they wish.

Have you ever heard cats—
Meowling "I'm hungry!
Give me a snack!"

Meowing "I'm lonely!
Give me a pat!"

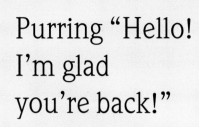

Purring "Hello!
I'm glad
you're back!"

Mewing and asking
"Did you hear that?"

Have you ever seen cats—
hissing and screaming
in anger or fright,
flicking their tails
from left to right,

baring their teeth,
ready to bite,
arching their backs
and ready to fight?

And have you seen
how cats stay clean
from head to tail
and in between?

With sandpaper tongues
all pink and rough
they comb their coats
till they're clean enough.

Have you seen the eyes of cats—
some green,
some gold,
some blue?
Some cats have eyes that do not match,
but most have pairs that do.

Did you know that cats can see
in very little light?
Have you seen their bright eyes glow
like sequins in the night?

Over their eyes,
under their chins,
on the sides of their faces
cats' whiskers grow in.
Wiry whiskers
sprout from their snouts
like extra paws
for feeling about.

And did you know
cats aim their ears
to listen for a sound?
And cats can hear
tiptoeing feet
that barely touch the ground.

Country cats, city cats,
pretty little kitty cats,
cats inside of houses,
cats inside of stores,
sitting on the windowsill
looking out of doors.

Cats in the barnyard,
cats up a tree,
so many kinds of cats
for you . . .

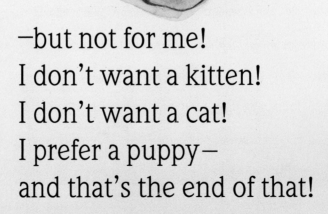

—but not for me!
I don't want a kitten!
I don't want a cat!
I prefer a puppy—
and that's the end of that!

EASY
0

Oppenheim, Joanne.

Do you like cats?

$18.60

XG5221433

DATE			